The Beautiful Christmas Tree

To Joan Palladino, with love
—C. Z.

To Max and Isabel
—Y. N.

Story copyright © 1972 by Charlotte Zolotow
Illustrations copyright © 1999 by Yan Nascimbene

The text of this book is set in 16-point Goudy.
The illustrations are watercolors, reproduced in full color.

Library of Congress Cataloging-in-Publication Data
Zolotow, Charlotte, 1915–
The beautiful Christmas tree / Charlotte Zolotow :
illustrated by Yan Nascimbene.
p.   cm.
Summary: Although his elegant neighbors do not appreciate his
efforts, a kind old man transforms his rundown house and small
neglected pine tree into the best on the street.
ISBN 0-395-91365-9
[City and town life—Fiction. 2. Trees—Fiction. 3. Christmas—
Fiction.] I. Nascimbene, Yan, ill.   II. Title.
PZ7.Z77Be   1999
[E]—dc21   98-50006   CIP   AC

Manufactured in the United States of America

HOR 10 9 8 7 6 5 4 3 2 1

The Beautiful Christmas Tree

Charlotte Zolotow
illustrated by Yan Nascimbene

HOUGHTON MIFFLIN COMPANY
BOSTON 1999

There once was a city street with a row of trees in front of the brownstone houses. It was a lovely street. Birds sang in the trees, people swept the stoops and sat there on hot summer nights enjoying the stars. All the houses were lived in except one. It had been empty for a long time.

The street with its trees and birds began to attract some very fashionable people. These new people did not sit out on their stoops. They were too elegant for that. None of them would buy the empty house. It was too rundown.

When Mr. Crockett moved in, it was plain that he was not fashionable. His neighbors saw him washing the dirty windows of the brownstone himself. "A peculiar man," they said, watching him scrub and polish until the windows shone and sparkled like a sheet of mountain air— fresh and clean.

One fall day they saw Mr. Crockett come out with a spading fork. He loosened the dirt in the little patch in front of his house. He dug his spading fork in and turned the ground. Then he let some of the dirt fall through his fingers. A fat worm squiggled its way back into the ground. He smiled.

"It's good earth; something will grow here," he said to himself.

The neighbors watched him walk happily up the stairs to his house and they shook their heads.

At the end of the street there was a flower shop. Coming home from work each night Mr. Crockett stopped to look in the window at the plants. The night before Christmas he stopped as usual to look in. There were lots of bright red poinsettias and many pots of little bushy pines.

But off in a dark corner of the shop he saw one wooden pot with a wizened little tree in it. Its branches drooped and dry needles had fallen on the floor.

Mr. Crockett couldn't help imagining how it would feel to be that small, misshapen tree among all the straight healthy bristly pines.

He opened the door to the shop and walked in. The florist came from the back of the shop.

"Good evening, sir," he said, "What can I do for you?"

Mr. Crockett was staring at the little tree.

"A nice poinsettia plant?" the florist suggested. "We have some beauties."

Mr. Crockett shook his head no, but before he could speak, the flower man went on, "A potted pine? We have some lovely ones left." And he picked up one of the bushy plants and held it out for Mr. Crockett to see.

"It's very fine," said Mr. Crockett, "but the plant I want is that little one in the corner."

"That one!" said the flower man.

"I can't really charge you for it. It's ugly."

Mr. Crockett smiled.

"I want to pay for it," he said. "There is an old saying," Mr. Crockett said as the flower man counted out his change. "Beauty is as beauty does. We'll see what this plant can do."

The bell tinkled overhead as Mr. Crockett opened the door to leave. Alone in the store, the flower man shrugged.

He'd have shrugged even more if he had heard Mr. Crockett talking to the tree as he walked along.

"You need sun," he told the tree, "and I know just the window for you," he said as though the tree could hear him. "And next spring we'll put you in the ground." Mr. Crockett knew a secret — living things need love and care.

That night the snow began to fall. On Christmas Day, when the neighbors went to church, they glanced at each beautifully decorated tree in the window of each brownstone until they came to Mr. Crockett's house. There was a brown pot in the window with a stick of a tree, crooked and almost without needles. "Awful!" they exclaimed.

Winter passed. The birds who flew south in the winter came back in the spring and joined the birds who had stayed.

One warm evening Mr. Crockett came out again with his spading fork. He loosened the earth in front of his house once more. He dug a deep hole and filled it with water. Then he brought out the stick of a tree.

Carefully he lifted the little pine out of the pot and set it gently in the hole. Then he poured more water around it so the roots floated comfortably into position. Then he packed the earth down around until the little pine stood firm in its new home.

The neighbors watching thought he was strange. "Stay away from that man!" they told their children. And the children did, except for a little boy named David who liked the good things Mr. Crockett did.

One evening Mr. Crockett noticed a small sparrow hopping about near his pine tree. It pecked the ground searching for food, but there was nothing there, and the next day Mr. Crockett brought out a bag of bread crumbs and sprinkled them around the tree.

Spring grew into summer. The hot sun beat down on the little tree. Mr. Crockett watered it each night and summer slowly turned to fall. The autumn wind turned cold.

More needles fell off the little pine and blew down the street. Mr. Crockett put hay around the base of the tree to protect it.

The first snow came. It powdered the street white. It covered the steps of the brownstones. It clung to the branches of Mr. Crockett's little pine. But the hay kept the tree's roots warm. The neighbors shook their heads when they saw Mr. Crockett sprinkling bread crumbs in the snow under the pine. "Foolish man," they said.

At last winter was over. The sun grew stronger. The days were longer. The smell of spring blew in on the soft country wind.

Mr. Crockett took away the hay.

The little tree was covered with clusters of blue-green needles that fanned out into dark green branches and made a shadow like an etching on the stoop of Mr. Crockett's house. The neighbors didn't notice. They didn't notice either that their own trees weren't quite as full as they used to be, and that there were not so many birds nesting in the branches of *their* trees. They didn't see that with the sparrows came red cardinals and their orange brides, grackles and a large white mourning dove, all to eat the food Mr. Crockett put out.

The neighbors didn't notice that the pine tree was growing taller and that everything about Mr. Crockett's brownstone shone clean and cared for, while slowly their own houses were losing some of the elegance they liked.

The children did notice. Especially David. He would stop on his way home from school and look at the unusual birds hopping around at the foot of Mr. Crockett's tree. Some evenings he came and sat next to Mr. Crockett on the stoop and they watched the birds together.

The summer passed. And fall came. And fall passed and winter came. And several years went by. David was growing into a young man. Mr. Crockett was older too. His curly beard was white and his shaggy eyebrows were white.

On a Christmas Eve, years after Mr. Crockett had moved onto the street and bought his tree, it began to snow. It snowed all night, covering the steps of the brownstones. It covered Mr. Crockett's house. It clung to the branches of Mr. Crockett's strong pine, and when it stopped snowing the white world sparkled like crystal. The carolers who usually passed Mr. Crockett's house almost went by. But David stopped them.

"We'll sing here, too," he said. And they sang. Their voices, beginning so suddenly, startled the birds eating under the pine and with a fluttering of wings they flew up into the tree.

At the very top the white dove lit, and the other birds with their colored feathers settled in the branches like living ornaments.

The carolers' voices, low and sweet, made the birds themselves begin to sing.

The carolers watched spellbound, looking at the snow-tipped tree bright with birds. And Mr. Crockett, behind his shining window upstairs, smiled at David and listened to the singing, carolers and birds together. It was a chorus of love, and Mr. Crockett knew this is what Christmas was meant to be.